Ambe

Follow all of Natty and Ned's adventures!
Collect all the fantastic books in the
Magic Pony series:

Magic Pony

Summer Dreams

Three magical books
in one!

ELIZABETH LINDSAY

Illustrated by John Eastwood

■SCHOLASTIC

Scholastic Children's Books
Euston House, 24 Eversholt Street,
London NW1 1DB, UK
a division of Scholastic Ltd
London ~ New York ~ Toronto ~ Sydney ~ Auckland
Mexico City ~ New Delhi ~ Hong Kong

A Dream Come True!
First published in the UK by Scholastic Ltd, 1997
Text copyright © Elizabeth Lindsay, 1997
Illustrations copyright © John Eastwood, 1997

Pet Rescue
First published in the UK by Scholastic Ltd, 1997
Text copyright © Elizabeth Lindsay, 1997
Illustrations copyright © John Eastwood, 1997

Night-Time Adventure
First published in the UK by Scholastic Ltd, 1997
Text copyright © Elizabeth Lindsay, 1997
Illustrations copyright © John Eastwood, 1997

This edition published in the UK by Scholastic Ltd, 2006

10 digit ISBN 0 439 950 87 2
13 digit ISBN 978 0439 950879

Printed and bound by Norhaven Paperback A/S

10 9 8 7 6 5 4 3 2 1

The right of Elizabeth Lindsay and John Eastwood to be identified respectively
as the author and illustrator of this work has been asserted by them in
accordance with the Copyright, Designs and Patents Act, 1988.

Magic Pony

A Dream Come True!

For Jo, with love and thanks.

Contents

Chapter 1
No Time for Pretends

Natty came down the garden path and opened the front gate. In the field on the other side of the lane, Penelope Potter's pony, Pebbles, was dozing in the sun. Yesterday, before Pebbles nearly ate it, Natty had found a four-leaved clover in his field.

Jamie said the clover was incredibly lucky and had tried to buy it, but that's brothers for you. Now it was taped on the wall above her bed, four round leaves and a stalk and, although its greenness was fading, Natty hoped its luck would grow and bring her the pony of her own she had always dreamed of.

There was no sign of Penelope, and Natty wondered if she had time for a secret pretend.

The pretend was to climb the gate, stroke Pebbles's soft nose and imagine he was hers.

"Hurry up, Jamie," Mum shouted from the front door. "We'll miss the bus." She spied Natty by the gate. "I can't think what he's doing."

Natty sighed a big sigh. The pretend would have to wait.

Jamie bounded out of the front door, slamming it behind him, and was at the gate in three leaps.

"Don't hang about," he said, giving Natty a dig. "What you waiting for?"

Jamie was jingling, his pockets full of birthday money, and Mum was taking him to the magic shop in town to spend it. Natty was having to tag along too, so she had brought her purse just in case.

Jamie was going to be a conjurer when he grew up, a fact he told everyone. He'd even made a flowing black cloak to prove it. Natty was going to be a famous horse rider, but she didn't yet know how. Mum and Dad couldn't even afford riding lessons, so owning her own pony was an impossibility. Would finding a four-leaved clover make any difference? She wondered. Mum put an arm around her shoulders and gave her a squeeze.

"Cheer up, Natty."

Natty managed a smile just as Penelope Potter cycled past on her gleaming new bicycle.

"Not going riding today, Penelope?" Mum asked.

"I am later," Penelope said. "When I've finished riding my bike."

A new bike *and* a pony, thought
Natty. It's people like Penelope who
have all the luck. And she trailed
after her mum and brother to the
bus stop.

It was market day in town and
they had to weave their way
between the busy stalls to Cosby's

Magic Emporium, Jamie's favourite shop. It was tucked down a little side street off the market square. The shop front was faded and the paint peeled.

By the time Mum and Natty arrived, Jamie had disappeared inside.

Natty peered through the dingy window and was about to follow Mum in, when something at the back of the display caught her eye.

"Coming Natty?" Mum asked.

"Can I look a minute?"

"If you like. I'll see what Jamie's up to."

Tucked behind the card tricks, spectacles with funny noses, itching powder, pretend blood, extraordinary hats and magic rope was a poster. A chestnut pony with a white star and blaze, wearing the cheekiest expression, looked Natty straight in the eye. Natty couldn't imagine what a pony poster was doing amongst all the jokes and magic tricks but it made no difference. She wanted that

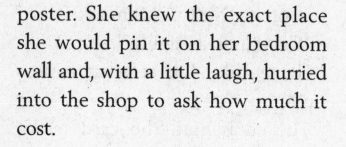

poster. She knew the exact place she would pin it on her bedroom wall and, with a little laugh, hurried into the shop to ask how much it cost.

Chapter 2

The Poster

The shop bell tinkled and Natty closed the door behind her. She stepped round two large cardboard boxes to where she could see Mum and Jamie watching an old man with gold-rimmed spectacles and wispy grey hair demonstrate a magic trick.

"Hocus pocus rim tin tiddle," he said and triumphantly held up what looked like an ordinary piece of rope.

Jamie gasped in admiration.

"That's brilliant! I saw you cut it up. I know I did." He took the offered rope and looked at it carefully. "I'll definitely take that trick."

The old man's eyes twinkled behind his spectacles.

"Thought you'd like that one."

"Natty, come and say hello to Mr Cosby." Mum waved at her to come forward.

"Interested in magic tricks are you, young lady?" the old man asked.

"Sort of," said Natty, not wanting to offend. "But I like ponies best. How much is the pony poster in the window, please?" Natty reached into her pocket for her purse.

"That pony needs a good home," said Mr Cosby, coming round from behind the counter. He shuffled past the cardboard boxes and opened what looked like a cupboard. When Mr Cosby took out the poster, Natty realized it was the door to the window display. "Four pounds."

"Four pounds!" Natty felt her hopes fade. She knew she didn't have four pounds.

Mum sighed. "Natty, are you sure you want another pony poster? It's a lot of money."

"Yes, I do. It's the most perfect picture. And if it was on my wall I could pretend it was my pony. We could have pretends together." She blushed. She didn't like talking about her pretends. Really they were a secret. She hurried to count out her money.

Mr Cosby closed the door to the cupboard that wasn't a cupboard and looked at the poster with satisfaction.

"This is the only one there is. There's not another like it." He walked back towards the counter and Natty was sure he whispered, "So you're very lucky to get it."

"Lucky?" said Natty. "Oh, yes, I am. The pony's so beautiful. I couldn't bear not to have him."

"Well, how much money have you got?" Mum asked.

"Three pounds twenty-seven pence," Natty replied, making a pile on the counter.

Jamie, who had been trying to work out the rope trick, suddenly took an interest.

"I've never seen horse posters here before."

"Don't usually get them," agreed Mr Cosby. "This is a one-off special just waiting for your sister."

"So how did you know we were coming?"

Mr Cosby smiled in a vague sort of way and, realizing he was not going to get a reply, Jamie went back to his rope trick.

"Mum, please can you lend me seventy-three pence?" Natty asked.

"Are you sure, Natty? It's all your pocket money gone in one go."

"Quite sure," said Natty, who would have paid even more if necessary.

"He's called Ned," said Mr Cosby. "I think you'll find him good value for money. In fact I know you will."

Natty put her three pounds twenty-seven in Mr Cosby's hand and Mum added seventy-three pence. Smiling up at Mr Cosby, Natty was sure he gave her a wink before rolling Ned into a tube and slipping on an elastic band.

"You look after him," he said, handing Ned over. "Find him a nice place on your wall and he'll look after you. He's all yours now."

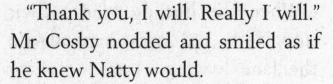

"Thank you, I will. Really I will."
Mr Cosby nodded and smiled as if
he knew Natty would.

On the bus going back Jamie
was impatient to get home, eager
to try out his new tricks. Natty
nursed her poster, thinking of
wonderful new pretends to have
with Ned. She was longing to take
another look at him.

When the bus drew into their stop, Natty and Jamie jumped into the lane leaving Mum to follow more slowly.

"If you're going to run on ahead," she said to Jamie, "take the key." And she handed it over.

Natty didn't run but did trotting steps, pretending to be on Ned's back.

When she got to the field gate, Penelope cantered past on Pebbles, turning him to jump a line of blue barrels. Natty would have stayed to watch, but the poster seemed to wriggle in her hand and remind her it was there. She didn't wait for Pebbles to jump the barrels again. She ran up the path to the front door and hurried in after Jamie. There was something important she had to do.

Chapter 3

The Pile on the Landing

Natty's feet clattered up the stairs and along the landing to her bedroom. It was the smallest room in the house – apart from the bathroom – and a bed, a chest of drawers, bookshelves and a desk were all that could be fitted in. Her hanging-up clothes went in the big wardrobe in Mum and Dad's bedroom. Sometimes, she minded that Jamie's room was twice the size, but he was the eldest and that was that. But she liked the view from her window, which included the whole of Pebbles's field and, from her bed, she was close enough to see Esmerelda, Prince and Percy, her three china ponies on the window sill and all her pony pictures on the wall.

Natty slipped off the rubber band and her new poster unrolled. Ned looked up at her from the duvet while she reached for her paper pins, hardly taking her eyes off Ned's chestnut face. Somehow he seemed bigger, more head and shoulders than she remembered him in Mr Cosby's shop.

There, she was sure, she had seen his back and the top of his tail. Now he was like a pony looking out over his stable door. Puzzled, she

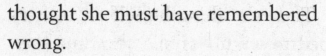

thought she must have remembered wrong.

But it didn't stop her wanting his head to pop out of the picture. Of course, it didn't – which was sad.

She pinned Ned up above the chest of drawers, the best place for Natty to see him without getting a crick in her neck.

Then she flung herself on to her bed to try it out and glimpsed the four-leaved clover, still taped to the wall above her head.

"You did bring me luck," she told it. "You brought me Ned." She lay back and gave the chestnut pony a good long look.

Slowly she closed
her eyes and
began a new
pretend. She
told it in
her head
and it went like this.

– *Me and Penelope Potter are best
friends. Not true in real life, but never
mind! I collect a head collar from
Penelope's tack room and Penelope is
there. Penelope says, "Hello, Natty.
Shall we go riding together?"*

*I say, "Yes, that would be nice. I was
just on my way to the field to bring
Ned in."*

Penelope says, "I'll come with you and fetch Pebbles."

Together we walk to the field gate and call.

"Ned!"

"Pebbles!"

The two ponies come trotting over.

One is a pretty chestnut with long
flowing mane, one white stocking and
a white star and blaze on his face. . .

Natty opened her eyes just to
check on the star and blaze.

Yes, Ned was looking straight at her. She had got it right. The white stocking she had made up, not being able to see his feet. She closed her eyes again.

– The other pony is a pretty dappled grey. In no time at all we fasten on the head collars and lead our ponies to their stables. I enjoy doing this because I am able to feed Ned juicy pieces of carrot and he nuzzles my pocket for more.

Natty sighed. What would they do next? Oh, yes, grooming.

– I am carefully bolting Ned's stable door when a voice calls me—

"Natty. Natty, come down at once. It's teatime. I'm not telling you again." It was Mum's cross voice getting in the way and not the nice pretend voice she had given Penelope. Natty screwed up her eyes but otherwise didn't move. She wanted to brush Ned's ginger coat and make it gleam. This was her first real pretend with him and she didn't want to stop.

"Natty!" Jamie banged on her door.

"What?"

"It's teatime. Mum says you got to come now."

"I will come."

"And if you don't I've got to make you."

"Go away, horrid boy. I'm coming."
Natty sat up with a groan.

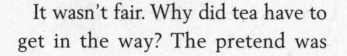

It wasn't fair. Why did tea have to
get in the way? The pretend was

going so well. On the other hand, she was feeling rather hungry. She swung her legs to the floor. Ned's eyes seemed to follow her to the door, which she liked.

"See you later," she whispered.

Downstairs in the living room the table had already been set. That was her and Jamie's job and she guessed Mum must have been calling for ages, got fed up and done it herself.

Dad wasn't back yet but Natty knew he would be soon. No wonder Mum was cross.

A key turned in the front door lock and the door slammed. It was Dad, and he came in looking really fed up.

"It's been one of those days," he said, slumping into a chair just as Mum came out from the kitchen.

"As bad as that, love?" she said, dropping a kiss on his forehead.

"I'll make you a nice cup of tea. Food'll be on the table in a couple of ticks."

They were just getting to the interesting bit of their meal, the cake course, when there was a startling crash, bang and gerflumph  from upstairs. Natty froze, cake halfway to her mouth, and listened.

If she hadn't known it was impossible she would have thought a large animal was clomping above their heads – like a cow or a horse. A horse!

She dropped the cake and made a dash for the door before anyone else even moved. Racing upstairs to her bedroom she found her duvet crumpled and all the books knocked on to it from the bottom shelf. And something else was wrong too. It took her a moment or two to work out what it was. Ned had disappeared. The poster was still there but, apart from a mass of blue sky, it was empty.

She stared astonished, until the rest of the family, pounding up the stairs, sent her running. The door into Mum and Dad's room was open and she peeped around it. Their bedspread was horribly crumpled too, although nothing else seemed different.

Then Natty noticed the funny smell. Everyone arrived at where it came from at the same time. Natty could hardly believe her eyes, for outside Jamie's room was a large pile of dung.

"Good grief," said
Dad. "Horse muck!"

Mum put her hands to her face.
"All over the carpet!" she wailed.

There was a moment's stunned silence, broken by something clumping in Jamie's room. Natty put her head round the door. A real live chestnut pony with one white stocking pawed at the carpet and swished his tail.

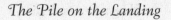

Natty gasped, eyes as round as pools. It was Ned.

"How did you get out of the picture?"

"I fell out. A mistake. I meant to jump." And he spoke!

Dad pushed the door open and in a blink Ned was gone. Natty couldn't work out where, until she saw a tiny pony trot along the window sill and hide behind the curtain.

Her brain worked fast. She saw that Jamie's black cloak had been trodden on and was ripped. What with that and the dung on the landing no one was going to be pleased that there was a pony loose in the house, especially one that went from big to small, and seemed to come out of a picture.

"Is this some kind of a joke, Natty?" Dad asked.

"No," said Natty. "No." She couldn't think how to explain the smelly pile on the landing. "But dung is very good for roses."

Mum was stony-faced.

"I don't know how that mess got here but I want it cleaned up at once, Natty. Do you understand?" For some reason everyone was blaming her.

"Yes," said Natty. "I'll do it straight away." For although no one knew it was Natty's poster pony, Natty didn't want them to find out if she could possibly help it.

This, she realized, was a dream come true and she just wanted everyone to go away so she could find out more about it.

Chapter 4

The Tussle on the Carpet

Natty hurried to the garden. She took the shovel from the coal bunker and the bucket from the greenhouse. Mum, Dad and Jamie had gone back to finish their tea which, under the circumstances, Natty found surprising. She knew it wasn't her who had dumped horse pooh on the landing and couldn't imagine why they all thought it was. In the end she decided it was lucky that they did, even though she had been told to go to her room after clearing up and was definitely in disgrace.

She shovelled the smelly pile into the bucket, and carried it downstairs and out through the back door. Unsure where to put it, she took it to the bottom of the garden and dumped it on the compost heap. She washed the shovel and swilled the bucket and put them away where she found them.

Back on the landing, she sniffed the carpet and squirted it with carpet cleaner. She scrubbed hard and, by the time she'd finished, the messed-up patch was as good as new and much cleaner than the rest of the carpet.

She nipped into her bedroom to check Ned's picture. Still empty!

Then remembering the rip in
Jamie's black cloak and Mum and
Dad's crumpled bedspread she
hurried to sort things out. Her own
room could wait until later.

It didn't take a moment to
straighten the bedspread, but the
ripped cloak would take some time
to mend. Thank goodness she did
sewing with Mrs Plumley from next
door, so she knew what to do. She
didn't have much time. Soon Jamie
would finish tea and, almost
certainly, come upstairs to practise
his magic tricks. She tiptoed across
to the window sill, expecting to find

the miniature Ned behind the curtain. But he wasn't there. No time to look for him now.

She hurried into Mum and Dad's room in search of some black cotton, pins and a needle. She found the workbox in the big wardrobe. As quickly as she could, Natty pinned the torn sides together and began to sew.

She was not quick enough. She was only halfway down the rip when there was an angry cry from Jamie's bedroom. Now he'd discovered his cloak was missing, what was she going to do? Own up, she supposed.

"What do you mean you ripped it?"

"I didn't exactly say I ripped it. I said it got ripped. It was an accident and I am sewing it up."

"You'd better had. You wouldn't like it if I ripped something of yours, like that soppy pony poster."

Jamie stomped out of Mum and Dad's bedroom. Natty was after him, grabbing him by the arm and pulling to stop him going into her room. She knew if he was angry he could do anything.

"Please," she wailed. "Please. I am mending it. I'm really sorry your cloak got ripped." She clung on, almost pulling off Jamie's sweatshirt while he kicked her bedroom door. Bang, bang, bang! She would not let him get to her poster. It would ruin everything. Jamie tried his hardest to shake her off. Then he took a deep breath and from his red and furious face came a loud yell.

"GERROFF!"

But Natty had no intention of gerroffing. She had got a grip and wasn't letting go. It took all her strength, every bit, and she just hoped that someone, Mum or Dad, would arrive before Jamie finally won, because he was bigger and stronger, and would win in the end. She gritted her teeth as Jamie pulled her across the carpet and pushed at her bedroom door. It started to open.

From out of the corner of her eye she saw something small and chestnut, with a flowing mane and tail, canter through the crack into her bedroom.

There was a shrill whinny and the door banged shut, pushing Jamie back so hard that he knocked Natty into a crumpled heap. Before she could get up, Jamie shoved all his weight against the door and Natty thought he had won. But the door wouldn't budge.

To save face, Jamie jutted his chin forward and leaned towards her.

"If my cloak isn't mended properly, now, this instant, I'll get that poster and rip it into a million pieces, you see if I don't."

"I am mending your cloak. You know I am and I'll finish it now. I promise."

"You'd better had." At last Jamie's temper was cooling and, feeling safer now her bedroom door was stuck, Natty hurried to finish the sewing.

"If you two don't pack it in I'm coming up to knock your heads together!" Dad shouted up the stairs.

But as they had already packed it in Natty hoped he wouldn't bother. She went back into Mum and Dad's room and sat on the bed, feeling trembly. She and Jamie didn't often have fights but when they did, it was always horrid.

Natty picked up the cloak and found the needle. She sewed with her best tiny stitches to make the rip show as little as possible, although she knew the cloak would never be quite what it had once been. If only ponies didn't have such hard feet.

And as soon as she thought of ponies her mind began to spin. How could a pony come out of a picture, grow to its proper size, and in the blink of an eye shrink to almost nothing? How could it speak?

It was almost too much to take in.

And as Natty's fingers sewed, another question popped into her head. How would she get back into her bedroom?

Chapter 5

The Pony under the Bed

The cloak was finished at last, and when Natty held it up the mend was hardly visible. Mrs Plumley would have been proud of her and even Jamie was impressed when she gave it back, although he tried not to show it.

"Mmm, not bad," he said, putting it on with a flourish which turned the cloak into great bats' wings. "Want to see a trick?"

"Not just now," said Natty. "I've got things to do."

"Like unjamming your bedroom door?"

"Oh, it's not jammed now," said Natty, crossing her fingers and hoping she was right. "Something got wedged under it."

She hurried out of Jamie's room before he decided to come and look. Outside her door she put her ear to the wood and listened.

The room sounded empty, so she turned the handle. The door glided open as it usually did, and she went cautiously inside.

Ned's pony poster was still a blank and there was nothing on the bed except the books knocked from the shelf. She quickly put them back. She searched on her window sill where Esmerelda, Prince and Percy stood in an undisturbed line, still looking across the front garden to Pebbles's field.

There was nothing on the chest of drawers, so where was he?

"Ned," she whispered. "Ned, where are you?" She got down on her hands and knees. Under the chest of drawers there was nothing but fluff.

She turned to the bed, lifting the duvet so she could get a proper look underneath it. "Ned, are you there?"

On the far side of the gloomy space she saw him trot in a circle and shake his head, then stop to paw the carpet before cantering towards her. He was the same size as Percy, the smallest of her china ponies. It was like having Percy come to life.

Natty kept quite still, her eyes gleaming as if she couldn't quite believe what she was seeing. When Ned reached her knee, he jumped and landed on her thigh. Before Natty realized what she was doing, she stroked his tiny back. There was a sharp blast of air and she was suddenly squashed against the bed with Ned towering above her, the size of Pebbles.

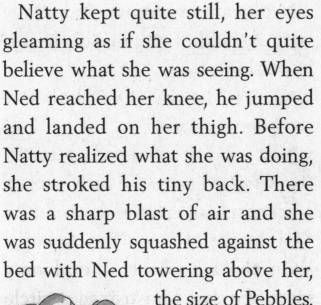

Ned was tacked up and ready with a saddle and bridle. It was astonishing.

"Get on," he said. "Quickly, before someone comes in."

Natty didn't need telling twice. She wriggled on to the bed, grabbed a handful of mane, and put a foot in the stirrup. The moment she was on his back a great wind blew. She shut her eyes against it.

When she opened them again she was clinging on like anything and Ned was cantering across a stretch of brown hillocks. He turned sharply around a large square tree and she nearly fell off. It took her a moment or two to realize that it wasn't a square tree but her bed leg, and that now she too had become tiny. She was wearing a hard hat and put a hand up to its silky smooth velvet, but not just that, she had on jodhpur boots, jacket, shirt and tie.

"I'm wearing riding things," she gasped, and couldn't imagine where her ordinary clothes had got to.

"Of course," said Ned. "Anyone ever teach you to ride?"

"Not really," said Natty. "When Penelope lets me, I walk about on

Pebbles. I have trotted twice but I've never really ridden."

"As I'm your magic pony, I shall teach you. That's what I'm here for."

"Yes, please," said Natty.

"Then take hold of the reins." Natty picked them up with one hand and kept hold of the mane with the other. Being small, she realized, meant it would be easy to learn to ride in her bedroom – there was masses of space. But Ned had other ideas, and trotted on to the landing. At the top of the stairs Natty gasped, for the drop looked huge.

"By the way," Ned said. "Tell your brother to keep his hands off my picture."

"Oh, he was cross about his magician's cloak, that's all," said Natty. "Now I've mended it, I'm sure he won't think of that again."

"It was lucky I managed to wedge the door shut in time. If that picture gets ripped that's the end of me."

"Oh, no!" said Natty.

"Oh, yes! So not a word to anyone about where I come from."

"Not a word. I promise." Natty clung on while Ned pawed at the carpet.

"Hold tight and off we go."

It was a shock when he jumped on to the first stair. Natty only just recovered her balance when he jumped to the next. She knew there were fourteen stairs and clung on grimly.

To her amazement, she was still on his back when Ned jumped to the hall floor. He trotted towards the living room, not seeming to mind Natty bouncing about like a sack of potatoes. Stretching high above them was the door, solid and thick, and open just enough for them to get through.

Mum and Dad were watching the television news, two giants sitting in mountainous chairs in front of a flickering screen. Spread across the carpet was a foot so big that Natty couldn't see to the other side. It was joined to a trousered leg that reached up for ever, or so it seemed.

"Fancy a canter across the carpet?" said Ned, setting off.

Knowing she was no bigger than a little mouse, Natty felt afraid. Then no sooner had she thought mouse than she thought cat.

"Tabitha!" From the kitchen came the bang bang of the cat flap. "Stop," said Natty. "There's Tabitha. . .!"

Before she could properly warn him, Ned took off, galloping across the carpet towards Dad's big foot. Instead of going round it, Ned jumped the foot in a great bound, landing with a thud that left Natty halfway up his neck.

The pony didn't stop but turned and raced to the kitchen, sliding to a standstill on the tiles.

In the middle of the floor, paw raised, for until that moment she had been washing it, sat Tabitha.

"I've been trying to tell you!" panted Natty, just about clinging on. "We've got a cat!"

Chapter 6
Cat Scare

Two green eyes gleamed and a fluffy tail twitched. Ned reared up and his front legs thrashed. Natty fell, the terrible wind a roar in her ears, and landed to her astonishment in the sink, her normal size again. Wedged in the washing-up bowl with her legs in the air, she struggled to pull herself out. There wasn't much room; Ned filled the kitchen. His tail swished, knocking cutlery from the draining-board and spice jars from the rack. He snorted at Tabitha and ignored the chaos of jars and cutlery smashing and crashing at his feet.

Such a shock turned Tabitha into a brush cat. Her coat stuck out in all directions. But not for long.

Dad burst into the kitchen. "What on earth's going on?"

Ned vanished and Natty felt for the give-away riding hat. That had gone too, and her ordinary clothes were back.

"For goodness' sake, Natty! Get out of the sink!"

"I can't."

 Natty scanned the floor for signs of Ned. So did Tabitha, who was beginning to get the hang of this creature who went from small to big and back again. She and Natty caught sight of Ned at the same time, as he cantered behind the vegetable rack and hid at the back of the rubbish bin. Tabitha pounced and batted behind the bin with her paw.

It was a relief to Natty to find Dad's strong arms at her shoulders, lifting her from the sink to the floor. She wriggled round Dad and grabbed Tabitha.

"Stop it, you," she said crossly, and unceremoniously dumped the struggling cat in the living room and shut the door.

Dad looked grimly at the mess of knives, forks and broken jars that scattered the floor.

"What is going on?"

"It was an accident," Natty said, feeling her wet bottom. "I'll clear it up."

"I should think you will," said Dad. "With the dustpan and brush. Mind you don't cut yourself on the glass."

"I'll get the dustpan." Before darting to the cupboard where the dustpan was kept, Natty opened the back door. She wanted Ned to escape to the garden and find a safer hiding place than behind the rubbish bin.

The moment Natty began to sweep, Mum opened the living-room door.

"Oh, what a mess!" she exclaimed.

Cat Scare

And not being a cat to miss an opportunity, Tabitha raced for the rubbish bin. Natty dropped the dustpan and dived. The rubbish bin went flying and through the hail of empty baked beans tins, wrappers and cartons, a tiny pony bolted for the garden. Tabitha scrambled from between Natty's arms and gave chase.

"Leave that cat alone," scolded Dad, stopping Natty in her tracks. "You're just making everything worse."

"The kitchen's a pigsty," said Mum. "Natty, how could you?" Natty didn't even try and explain. With one eye on the back door she righted the rubbish bin and swept as fast as she could.

Ages later the kitchen was clean again, and Natty hurried to put the dustpan away. There was no sign of Ned or Tabitha.

"Can I go now?" she asked.

"Yes," said Mum. "Straight up to bed and get those wet jeans off."

"But—"

"You heard what I said."

Natty knew there was no arguing, so after a quick peep out of the back door she hurried back through the living room and upstairs. Only instead of going to her bedroom, she went to the bathroom where she closed and locked the door.

The bathroom window opened out above the kitchen roof. Natty had never actually climbed out from here before, but Jamie had. Jamie had reached the ground that way. If he could do it, so could she.

Natty put down the toilet lid and climbed on to it. Then with a foot in the hand basin she balanced her knee on the window sill and opened the window.

From there she scanned the garden for signs of Ned and Tabitha. Washing hung limp on the line and the shed door was open. She would have to be careful. The twitch of a tabby-cat tail drew her eye to the canopy of rhubarb leaves billowing out from the vegetable patch. Tabitha, it seemed, was underneath.

Natty pulled herself up and perched in the open window. Turning, she eased herself down, hooking her arms over the sill until her toes touched the tiles of the kitchen roof. She had made it.

Crouching low she decided the best way to the ground was by the old trellis nailed to the wall at the far end. She crawled along the tiles and let herself down carefully.

Hoping she could not be seen from the living room, she hurried down the path, ducked under the washing, and crouched to peer under the rhubarb. It was a dark, dense, stalk-filled forest. Ned, if he was there, could be hiding anywhere. Tabitha's green eyes glinted.

"You leave Ned alone, Tabby," she

warned. "He's a pony, not a mouse." Tabitha blinked but her tail twitched just the same. "Ned, are you there?"

There was a thump and a clump and a bang.

"I'm here." The voice didn't come

from under the rhubarb, it came from the shed, where Ned's head peeped out, proper pony size, just as if he was looking out from a stable.

"What are you doing in there?" Natty asked.

"Hiding, of course. What do you think?"

Natty ran to the shed and put her arms round Ned's neck. She was so pleased he was safe! Then she noticed the saddle and bridle had gone. She looked around for them. On the floor lay Dad's claw hammer and wooden mallet.

"Sorry, I knocked the tools off with my bottom," said Ned. Natty picked them up and put them on the workbench.

"But where's the saddle and bridle?"

"They come and go when I don't need them," said Ned. "Just like your riding things."

"So it's real magic then," said Natty, eyes wide.

"Hat, boots, jacket, saddle, bridle, it's all real magic, including me!" Ned gave her an affectionate push with his nose.

"And now you've found me you can help me get back to my picture.

That's enough excitement for one day. Ready to carry me?"

"But I can't!"

"Yes, you can." And, in the blink of an eye, Ned was his tiny self, trotting across the floor.

Natty scooped him up in cupped hands and, with a quick look to check no one was watching, hurried to the trellis.

She balanced Ned on her shoulder
and slowly climbed, one foot then
the next, arms pulling until they
reached the roof. Here Ned jumped,
landing neatly in the gutter. He
trotted along the black gully, leaping
the leaves and twigs that had
collected there.

Natty crawled beside him across the tiles. She was beginning to think they would make it without further mishap, until she looked up and saw Tabitha crouched on the window sill. Ned scrambled from the gutter and Tabitha flew at him, claws unsheathed. In a trice Ned was big again, balancing dangerously on the slippery tiles. With a terrific effort he leaned back on his hocks and jumped for the bathroom window.

Natty put her hands over her ears, expecting to hear the crash and splinter of breaking glass, but there was only a silence, broken by Tabitha scuttling from the roof, her confidence shaken. Quickly, Natty put her hands over the window sill and hauled herself up. She tumbled into the bathroom in time to see the tiny Ned cantering across the bathmat. She managed to close the window before an angry banging started on the door.

"Hurry up, Natty. You've been ages. What are you doing in there?"

It was Jamie, fed up with waiting.

"Coming," said Natty, undoing the lock. But before she had a chance to pick Ned up, the door was pushed open and Jamie barged in.

"You're not the only one who wants to get ready for bed." Ned shied sideways and galloped for the landing.

"Sorry," said Natty and rushed after him.

"So I should think." And the bathroom door slammed without Jamie noticing a thing.

Inside her bedroom, Natty closed the door and ducked down to look for Ned under the bed. He wasn't there. Neither was he on the window sill or under the chest of drawers. It was only when she sat on her bed that she saw he was back in the poster. She sighed a huge sigh of relief.

But a picture pony cannot talk, and as Natty pulled off her wet jeans and pulled on her dry pyjama bottoms she began to miss him.

"Ned? Did you really happen?" she asked, running a finger across the poster's shiny surface. It was cool and only paper, not a bit like the warm silky fur she longed to feel.

She sat back on the bed and stared up at him.

"We had an adventure, didn't we?" she said at last. "A scary one." But already she wasn't quite sure. It could have been a pretend, except she'd never have thought up such an exciting one.

Mum came in to kiss her goodnight.

"Night night, love," she said, stroking Natty's hair. "Lost in a dream as usual."

"Not really." Natty smiled. "At least, I don't think so."

"Well if you aren't, you soon will be. Have sweet ones," said Mum. "See you in the morning."

It was after Mum closed the door that Natty noticed a long chestnut hair on her duvet. She picked it up and her heart beat fast with excitement. It must have come from Ned's tail.

"It is true," she said. "You did happen." Natty looped the hair carefully over her four-leaved clover so that it hung above her on the wall. Then she snuggled down.

Maybe, just maybe, Ned would come to life again soon and, with that wish on her lips and her fingers crossed to make it come true, she fell fast asleep.

The End

Magic Pony

Pet Rescue

For Jessamy, with love.

Contents

Chapter 1

Visitors

Natty lay stretched out on her bed, hands behind her head, with her tabby cat, Tabitha, a purring ball on her chest. Drifting into a wonderful pretend, Natty imagined Ned, the chestnut pony in the poster on her wall, jumping from his picture.

– "Take me on an adventure, Ned," she said, climbing on to his strong back. "Like you did before!" With a whoosh and whirl of magic wind, they are in the field on the other side of the lane. Here Penelope Potter's *pony Pebbles watches in astonishment as they soar over a line of blue barrels, the very barrels Pebbles jumps so often with his owner. And Natty doesn't wobble once, for in a pretend everything goes according to plan and she never ever falls off.*

There was a big sigh and Natty opened her eyes, gently toppling Tabitha on to the duvet, before sitting up. Tabby curled into the warm space left behind and promptly fell asleep. Natty swung her feet to the floor, gazed at Ned's picture and sighed another sigh, one of loss and longing.

It seemed like for ever ago that she had bought the pony poster at Cosby's Magic Emporium.

A long, chestnut hair from Ned's tail hung on the wall above her bed. The hair wasn't pretend, it was real, and Natty knew in her heart of hearts that Ned could still come out of the poster – even if the magic had worked only once so far. Maybe, when Jamie next went to buy a magic trick, she should go too and ask Mr Cosby if she had to do something special to make the magic happen.

She stood up to touch the cool, shiny paper and ran a finger along Ned's white blaze.

"Are you going to come alive again? Are you?" she asked, but nothing changed and there was not the slightest hint that Ned was anything other than a pony in a picture.

Natty turned to her three china horses on the window sill. Esmerelda had her back to Prince and Percy.

Now Natty rearranged them into a nose-to-nose huddle so they could talk to each other, unaware that the head in the poster had turned, just a little, to follow what she was doing.

"Esmerelda, Prince, Percy – I'm going on an adventure. Tell Ned to come too?" But the three china horses were silent.

It was no good. She would have to adventure on her own. Natty grabbed an invisible rein, jumped on to a chestnut back that wasn't there and set off at a canter to the top of the stairs. Then clumpity, clumpity, clumpity all the way down to the bottom, riding like the wind. Her thumping feet brought Mum hurrying from the living room.

"Natty, that's an awful lot of noise. I thought you'd fallen downstairs." Natty jogged on the spot; her pony prancing. "If you've got nothing better to do, Jamie's outside and might like some help. He's going to make Fred disappear."

Natty shook her head. "He'll never do it."

"I have my doubts too," admitted Mum. "But he insists on trying. Why don't you give him a hand?"

It was true that Jamie's conjuring was getting better and his latest card trick was brilliant. But he didn't stand a chance of making a goldfish vanish, let alone a goldfish in a bowl. No, she'd got better things to do than get involved with that.

"I'll just say hello to Pebbles," Natty said, and cantering to the front door, she reared up to undo the latch. "And Penelope if she's there." Mum smiled and left her to it.

Natty trotted down the garden path to the front gate. Ned would jump it with an easy leap and a swish of his tail. If she tried it,

common sense told her she would
end up flat on her face. If only he
would come out of his poster.

Reaching the other side of the
lane, Natty reined in her invisible
pony and dismounted. She put her
foot on the middle rung of the field
gate, hoisted herself
up and leaned
over.

She was just in time to see Penelope lead Pebbles out of the far gate to his stable. Natty swung herself to the other side and, landing on her invisible pony's back, set off at a gallop across the well-cropped grass.

"Whoa boy, whoa," she said, arriving at the far gate. Breathing hard, she let herself into the small stable yard and set her pretend pony free.

"Hello, Penelope. Need any help?"

Penelope, who was tying Pebbles's halter rope to the string on the ring outside his stable, considered the offer.

"You can groom him if you like. You can't ride him though. My cousin Daisy's going to do that. I'm getting him ready for her."

"Your cousin?" Natty enquired, eager to get her hands on a brush before Penelope changed her mind.

"Daisy, Auntie Peg and Uncle Ralph are staying for the weekend. They're back at the house. I've come over to get Pebbles ready. Daisy's younger than me so I'm looking after her."

"That's nice," said Natty, fetching Pebbles's red-bristled dandy brush, ready to start. Penelope held up the pony's yellow stained tail and wrinkled her nose.

"It'll have to be washed, Pebbles.

Daisy can't ride you with a tail like that."

"Not a good idea," agreed Natty, happily, for if Penelope was busy tail-washing it meant she could brush away to her heart's content. She began at once on the pony's dappled grey neck. Pebbles stood like a rock with eyes half closed.

He was particularly itchy around the ears and when Natty scratched them he leaned into her hand and wobbled his bottom lip. She scratched harder. Wobble, wobble, wobble went the lip.

In the end Natty's fingers ached so much she had to stop and Pebbles was heard to breathe a sigh of regret.

She brushed his neck, his back, his tummy, his front and rear legs – and that was just one side. By the time Penelope arrived with a bucket of hot water, Natty was dust-covered and puffed.

"Not bad," said Penelope. "You've missed a bit there though, and don't forget to comb his mane."

Natty nearly said, And what did your last slave die of? but stopped herself. She didn't want to fall out with Penelope, not when she was to be allowed a go with the mane comb. She changed sides and brushed and brushed, while Penelope plunged the dirty tail into the hot water. Pebbles was quite used to all this and carried on dozing, not minding at all when Penelope squeezed on a large dollop of horse shampoo and got down to a thorough rubbing. Soon his tail was a mass of dirty brown foam.

"Fill a bucket, Natty. I need to rinse it."

Natty put down the dandy brush and surveyed her work. Only the mane to do. But first, Madam Penelope wanted water. Honestly! Hadn't she heard of the word please?

Natty staggered back from the tap with a bucketful, only to be told to get another.

"I need loads," said Penelope. "To get all the soap out."

Dutifully, Natty filled another bucket. She was about to rummage in the grooming box for the mane comb when a car reversed down Penelope's drive, across the lane and into the little yard.

"Here they are," cried Penelope, whirling the dripping tail round and round and showering Natty.

"Hey, do you mind!"

"Natty, get rid of the buckets,"
Penelope ordered, thrusting two at
her. "I'll quickly do his mane."

"But I was going to do that!"

Penelope ignored her.

Fed up, Natty dumped the buckets
in the tack room. There wasn't
much point in hanging about only
to be in the way, so she started for
the gate.

A girl, with a mass of blonde
curls and wearing a new pair of
jodhpurs and gleaming jodhpur
boots, climbed from the car. Must
be Daisy, thought Natty, and
she watched from the top of the

gate, envying the little girl her smart
new riding clothes.

The man – Uncle Ralph, Natty
supposed – opened the back of the
car and revealed a brown hutch.

"Get the other end, Daisy."

"It's too heavy by myself," said
Daisy.

Penelope glanced at Natty. Natty
took the hint.

"I'll help," she said, jumping from
her perch.

Daisy and Natty got one end and Uncle Ralph the other and between them they lifted out the hutch. They were about to place it on the concrete when the hutch door swung open.

"Careful, Flopper will get out," said Daisy.

But, as Natty realized on closer inspection, whoever or whatever Flopper was, he had already got out, for the hutch was empty.

Chapter 2

The Face at the Window

Natty quickly learned that Flopper was Daisy's pet rabbit. The most perfect, snow white creature in the whole world, with a name to match his ears.

"They flop sideways," sobbed Daisy, twisting Flopper's red lead in her hands. "And his paws are pink and his nose is pink and it twitches. You'll know him the moment you see him." But since Flopper appeared gone for ever, Daisy's sobs became heartbroken wails.

Daisy and her parents had arrived late yesterday evening, Natty was told. It had been too dark to find a place out of doors for Flopper to spend the night, so they had left him in the back of the car, locked in his hutch – or so they thought. Uncle Ralph had left a gap in the back door to make sure Flopper had plenty of fresh air.

But now, when they wanted to take him for a walk in Pebbles's field, he was gone, already walking himself goodness knows where.

Penelope clasped her hands over her ears, trying to cut out Daisy's agonizing cries.

"I'll look for him," said Natty, understanding that if Flopper were her pet rabbit she would be feeling just like Daisy.

"Look anywhere you like," said Penelope. "But a rabbit on its own all night in our garden will certainly have been eaten by the fox."

Daisy's cries became instantly worse and Uncle Ralph looked even more worried. Natty thought it best not to mention that Tabitha had also been known to bring home the occasional rabbit. Instead, she tried to be of comfort.

"He may have found a nice little hole to hide in. He may have gone visiting and met up with other rabbits." At this crumb of hope, Daisy's wails lessened.

"Do you think so?" she asked, between sobs.

"It's possible."

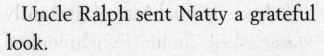

Uncle Ralph sent Natty a grateful look.

"Anyway," said Natty. "I'll get going. I'll look in the lane, in Mrs Plumley's front garden, in ours and in the wood."

"Where will we look, Penelope?" Daisy asked, looking brighter now that positive action was to be taken.

"Our garden and the field, I suppose." Penelope sighed. "Both are huge; it'll take ages."

Natty waved goodbye. Her search would start straight away. She hurried past Uncle Ralph's shiny car and once out of sight, jumped upon her invisible pony and trotted into the lane. She looked this way and that. No white rabbit was to be seen.

Turning towards home, Natty reached next door's house first. She peered over the garden gate.

Nothing on the grass. Not a glimmer of white fur amongst Mrs Plumley's prize dahlias or behind the willowy hollyhocks. At the next gate, her own, a soft burbling sound, the sort horses make by blowing through their noses, brought her to an abrupt stop.

"Hello, down there!"

Natty looked up and cried out with delight. Ned, the pony in the poster, was alive again. He leaned from her bedroom window as if over a stable door. She quickly looked round to make sure no one else was witness to this extraordinary sight.

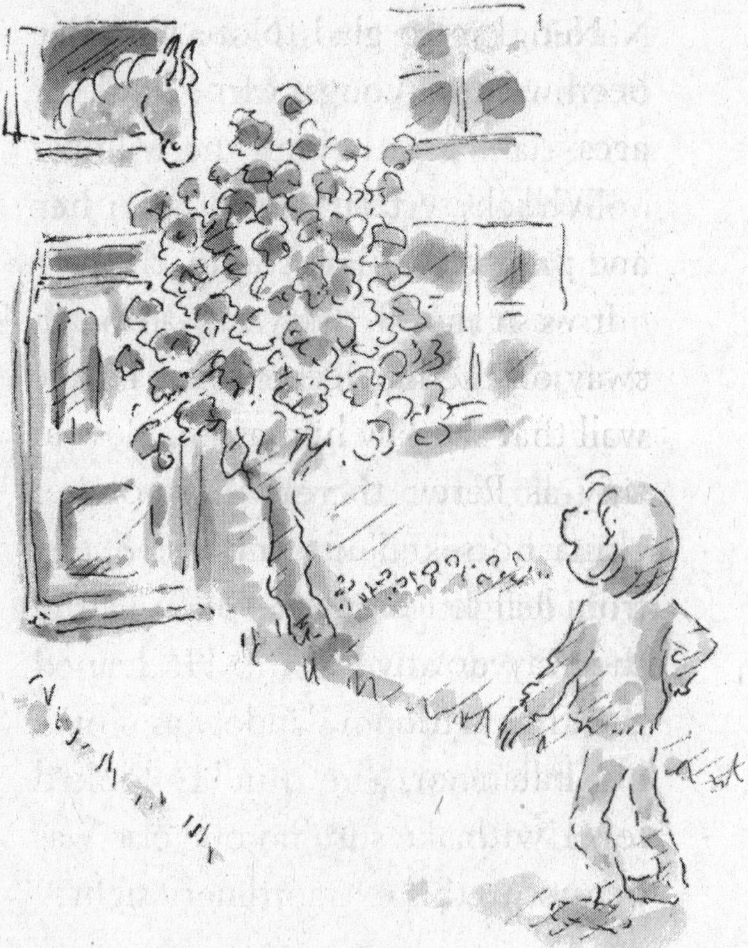

"Ned, I'm so glad to see you. I've been wanting you to come back for ages."

"Well, here I am," said the pony and promptly disappeared.

It wasn't until Natty saw a branch sway on the fig tree growing by the wall that she saw him again. Now as tiny as Percy, the smallest of her china horses, Ned sprang from leaf to leaf all the way down the tree until he balanced level with her nose.

"Help me down then and we'll go for a ride." His little voice reminded her of tinkling bells.

"A ride! Oh, Ned, I'd love to, but I'm looking for a lost rabbit."

"A lost rabbit, eh? I'll help you look."

With glowing eyes, Natty reached up two flat palms for Ned to climb on to, then carefully lowered him to the ground.

In the time it takes to blink, he was at her side, big and strong, the size Pebbles had been when she'd groomed him, wearing a bridle and a saddle, ready for her to mount.

Natty took hold of the reins and swung herself on to his back. The moment her seat touched the saddle, sweatshirt, jeans and trainers were gone. In their place was a hacking jacket, jodhpurs and brown boots; underneath the jacket a shirt and tie. Her hands wore pale riding gloves and on her head was a velvet hard hat.

"I love the riding clothes! I could be Penelope Potter going to a horse show!" she exclaimed.

"You could indeed," said Ned, and he pulled the gate open with his teeth and went into the lane.

"Now where shall we look?"

"In Winchway Wood. It's this way. Turn left." Ned did so. "The rabbit's called Flopper and is completely white. He escaped in Penelope's garden."

Ned snorted and his trotting feet made delicate clicks on the road's hard surface; for, unlike Pebbles, he wore no shoes. It was strange not to hear the ring of metal.

Natty did her best up-down, up-down rising trot until they reached the path that led into the wood where the lane ended.

"Be careful, Ned. Lots of people walk their dogs this way. We mustn't be seen!"

"Don't worry. Just say hello and on we'll go."

"But you're a secret!"

"Where I come from is a secret. That you and I can become tiny is a secret. When we're ordinary like this, it doesn't matter so long as no one recognizes who you are."

"But they might."

"Dressed like that you have the perfect disguise. And, of course, I shall never speak when someone is near!" Ned's confidence in the riding clothes as a disguise made Natty long to look at herself in the mirror. She pulled her chin-strap straight and sat tall, feeling a different person.

"Hold on tight," said Ned. "And keep a lookout for that bunny."

Natty twisted some mane around her fingers just in case and Ned broke into a canter. To her delight, Natty found she hardly wobbled at all.

"You're getting better," cried Ned. "I told you I'd teach you to ride. Do you remember?" Natty did remember. "Don't you worry about a thing. Relax and it's as easy as breathing. You can leave the steering to me."

Natty did just that, enjoying herself utterly, her eyes darting here and there, ever on the lookout for a white rabbit. Ned cantered beneath the stately beech trees, his hooves beating out a steady rhythm on the path. A log lay ahead and Natty knew he was going to jump it.

"Don't worry, you'll hardly notice we've left the ground," Ned cried. The log came closer and the nearer they got the bigger it looked, but Ned made nothing of it. They flew over it and Natty stayed on even when they thudded to the ground on the other side.

A bubble of laughter burst from her. Jumping was fun.

Now Ned galloped, ears flat back, his mane flying, while the wind forced tears from Natty's eyes and whistled in her ears.

Then suddenly there was a dog, small and white, barking ferociously.

173

It came at them without warning. Ned shied off the path, made a whiplash turn and raised a forefoot, ready to confront the foe. Natty landed halfway up his neck.

"It's Ruddles," she gasped, clinging on. "Sit, Ruddles! Sit and stay!"

The little dog stopped, cocked his head on one side and sat, wondering how this stranger knew his name. Natty hauled herself back into the saddle. "Ruddles lives next door." The little dog raised an ear and waited expectantly. "Mrs Plumley must be taking him for a walk. Look, here she comes."

Stout Mrs Plumley waddled down the path towards them, waving Ruddles's lead.

"Ruddles, come here you little varmint," she called. "You leave that pony alone."

"Let's go, Ned," said Natty. "If she recognizes me, she'll certainly tell Mum and then I'll have some explaining to do."

"I've already told you, you have the perfect disguise," said Ned. "It's a good time to try it out. But remember, if you get off, don't let go of the reins or the riding clothes'll vanish."

Natty crossed her fingers and wished for luck.

"Good dog, Ruddles. Good boy," said the old lady, puffing up and stooping to clip on the lead. She smiled up at Natty. "Sorry about his barking, dear. He's a noisy so and so but he don't mean no harm." Natty smiled back but didn't say anything.

"You've got a pretty pony there. A lovely chestnut colour. What's his name?"

Natty swallowed nervously.

"Ned."

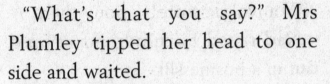

"What's that you say?" Mrs Plumley tipped her head to one side and waited.

"He's called Ned!"

"And a right handsome Ned he is too," said Mrs Plumley, patting Ned's sleek neck. "Well, I must be getting on. Come along, Ruddles. Enjoy your ride, me dear."

"Thank you," said Natty. "I will." And she breathed a huge sigh of relief as Mrs Plumley pulled the reluctant Ruddles on down the path.

"There," said Ned. "It's just as I said."

"It is," said Natty, grinning hugely.

"It's a real disguise."

Ned raised his head and stepped out in a businesslike way.

"Let's get on with this search," he said. "We've got a white rabbit to find."

Chapter 3
Rabbit Search

Ned trotted between the trees, twisting round the solid trunks. Natty scanned the ground at either side while Ned kept a forward lookout. From grassy patches the grey wood-dwelling rabbits hurried and scurried, flashing bobtails as they hid down holes and disappeared between tree roots. But a snow white rabbit with pink nose and paws was nowhere to be seen.

For all their looking hither and thither, Natty and Ned could only reach one conclusion – Flopper was not in Winchway Wood.

"Well, you can't say we haven't looked," said Natty. "We must have covered every bump, dip, nook and cranny."

"We certainly have." Ned came to a stop and blew a burbling pony sigh. "It's been a good ride but I say we go home."

Ned turned for the path and Natty was filled with a certain sadness. She loved being on Ned's strong back; already he was a real friend. But she was concerned for Flopper.

"I hope Penelope was wrong when she said a night out for Flopper meant the fox would get him."

Ned blew again, pursuing a thought.

"He's found somewhere more rabbit-friendly, that's what he's done." And he stretched his long neck.

"What's more rabbit-friendly than a wood full of rabbits?" wondered Natty.

"A garden full of cabbages, lettuces and juicy peas!"

"Of course," said Natty. "Grass must be boring for a rabbit that's used to treats. I bet Daisy gives him lots."

"I'm sure she does," agreed Ned.

"Like Mrs Plumley gives Pebbles a carrot every day. He likes it so much he waits by the gate."

"There you are then."

"Well," said Natty. "The nearest place to Penelope's garden where a rabbit can find all those treats is our vegetable patch."

"Mmm! Better take a look," said Ned.

"But he can't get in. Dad knows all about rabbits. There's netting right round the whole garden." Natty drew her eyebrows together. "I keep thinking he might have gone the other way, to the main road, and got himself squashed by a passing car. That would be terrible."

"It certainly would be," agreed Ned, trotting forwards. "The sooner we find out what's happened to him the better. We'll search the garden next."

They reached the path and ahead of them lay the log. Ned cantered towards it. His jump was effortless, although his rider slipped sideways. He stopped so Natty could straighten up.

"It was going downhill," she said, excusing herself and adjusting her hat.

"You're doing very well, very well indeed for a first ride out of doors."

They continued along the path and out of the woods, reaching Natty's house in a matter of moments.

"We'd better go round by the side gate," she said, dismounting. "There's less chance of bumping into anyone." Keeping hold of the reins she twisted round to admire her smart jodhpurs and shiny jodhpur boots.

"It would be best if you carry me," said Ned.

Natty knew her wonderful clothes would disappear the moment she let go. She closed her eyes. . .

"One, two, three!" . . . and dropped the reins. When she opened them again, Ned and the riding clothes had disappeared and she was back in her grubby jeans, sweatshirt, and boring old trainers.

But she brightened up when the tiny Ned trotted round her toes and she bent down with both hands outstretched.

He jumped neatly on to her palms and she lifted him carefully. Keeping her hands steady, Natty pushed the gate open with her bottom and slipped down the path to the back garden.

The first person she saw was Jamie. His conjuring gear was spread higgledy-piggledy across the grass and he was balancing his magician's top hat on a finger and holding his magic wand aloft. The goldfish bowl was sitting on the little table from the living room and Fred, fluttering his fins, was staring out at the flowers.

"Abracadabra, vroom, vroom vanish!" Jamie spun the hat on to his head and twirled his cloak. Fred, bowl and table were enveloped in blackness while Jamie began some kind of awkward struggle.

"Natty, be my assistant and I can do it," said Jamie, catching sight of her.

"Do what?" Natty asked, although she knew the answer.

"Make Fred disappear. I can't do it on my own because of the water. Every time I try I tip the bowl."

He uncovered the goldfish who was swimming round and round in frantic haste.

"Poor Fred, you're scaring him," said Natty. "Anyway that's cheating. It's not magic if you've got to get someone else to do it for you."

"Of course it's not cheating. Conjuring is sleight of hand, illusion and all that. An assistant just helps. What have you got there?"

Natty had been carrying on this conversation with her hands held out.

"Oh, nothing." And indeed, when she looked there was nothing. She shook them out to show this was true and at the same time glanced round. Much to her surprise it was Ned who'd vanished, although Natty knew it had nothing to do with Jamie's conjuring. Ned was hiding.

There was a distracting bang, crash and yelp in the shed and Dad danced into the garden holding his thumb. Natty rushed to see what the matter was, along with Mum, who ran from the kitchen.

"What's happened?" they both asked. Dad puffed and blew and, in an effort not to say rude words, went red in the face.

"I think it's his thumb," said Natty.

"Must have hit it with the hammer," said Jamie.

Dad let out a groan of a breath. "You could say that!"

"Bad luck," said Mum, gently lifting his hand to look. "Best run cold water on it to stop the bruising."

Natty leaned her face against Dad's arm. "Poor Dad. I hope it doesn't hurt too much."

"At least your thumb's still there," said Jamie, cheerily.

Dad ignored that remark and went indoors.

"OK, you two, it's teatime," said Mum. "Stop what you're doing and come in. And don't leave that fish outside in case the cat gets it."

"Natty, can you bring Fred?" Jamie asked, dropping his cloak and hat in a pile and offering the bowl expectantly.

"Why can't you?" grumbled Natty.

"I need two hands for the table." Natty took the bowl, taking care not to slop any water, and peered at Fred. He seemed calmer now he'd stopped being shaken about, and he peered back.

Having to go in for tea was a real nuisance. Natty wanted to find Ned and look for Flopper. Fed up, she followed Jamie and the table indoors.

Natty was glad to get Fred safely back in his place on the bookshelf and, while Mum came in with a plate of sandwiches, she took a quick look out of the window. She hoped that Ned, wherever he was, realized she had been dragged in for tea.

Mum returned to the kitchen to collect the teapot.

"Natty, there's a cake on the side. Come and fetch it for me, will you?"

Having got as far as the kitchen, Natty was tempted to sneak outside but when she saw that the cake was a yummy chocolate one she carried it into the living room.

"When did you make this?" she asked.

"I didn't. Mrs Plumley did. It's a thank you for keeping an eye on things while she's away."

"But she's not away."

"She will be tomorrow. She and Ruddles are going to town to stay with her sister for a few days."

"After tea I'll cut her a couple of lettuces and pull her some carrots to take," said Dad.

"She'd appreciate that," nodded Mum. "Carrots you buy never taste as good as the home-grown ones. Plates, Natty. Pass Dad a sandwich, Jamie." Natty gave Dad a plate and Jamie obediently offered the sandwiches.

"Wow, your thumb's going yuck red. I bet the nail comes off."

"Don't sound so excited," said Dad.

"What were you doing anyway?" Mum asked.

"There's a hole to mend. Some animal's pushed its way through the fence."

A hole in the fence! Natty's mind raced. Did that mean that Flopper was in the garden after all? She wished Mum would get on and cut the cake. She wanted to go and look.

"Now Jamie, tell me. . ." asked

Mum, sipping her tea and taking ages to get to the point. Natty fiddled impatiently with a sandwich. "Did you make Fred disappear?"

Jamie's face took on a look of despair.

"I need a rabbit. You can't do conjuring with a goldfish. The water tips out. Every magician should have a rabbit."

"And white doves," added Natty. "To pull from sleeves and top hats."

"Don't encourage him," said Mum. "A cat and a goldfish are plenty enough pets for one family."

"Don't even think of a rabbit," joined in Dad. "Garden pests, they are."

Natty fidgeted in her chair, aware that Flopper might be being a garden pest right now. Jamie scowled with disappointment.

At last Mum slid a knife through
the gooey chocolate cake.

"Pass your plate, Natty."
Natty bit into the dark stickiness,
lumpy with chocolate chips and
gooey with cocoa cream filling.

It was bliss. She chewed quickly to the last mouthful when a loud whinny from the garden startled her into action. Ignoring the protests from Mum and Dad, she swallowed, plonked down her plate and ran.

It was Ned calling; she had to go.

Chapter 4
The Thief in the Garden

Natty charged out of the back door and raced down the path. Was she looking for a big Ned or a little Ned? She didn't know. When she got to the shed she found the big Ned behind it, tacked up and waiting. She knew what to do. She reached for his withers and vaulted.

"Well done," said the pony, and the moment she was astride a wild wind spun them away, leaving his voice an echo. When it was calm again it seemed as if they were in a different place. The wooden wall beside them climbed for ever and feet the size of cars thudded along the vast plain of the path.

Natty cried out and clung on, while Ned cantered towards the dark space beneath the shed's floor. The black soles of Jamie's trainers rose above them, smacking down to miss them by a hair's breadth.

Ned swung round and together they peered out. More giant feet arrived and Natty recognized Dad's boots.

"Which way did she go, Jamie?" Dad's voice boomed out.

"I don't know. But I bet she's chasing after Penelope Potter on Pebbles. She's only got to hear a horse and she's gone."

"She's a cheeky little so and so running off like that in the middle of tea. Still, while I'm out here I'll pull those carrots for Mrs Plumley. Fetch me a bag will you?"

The feet clumped slowly away in different directions.

"Sounds like I'm in trouble," said Natty.

"And so's that rabbit!" nodded Ned.

"Have you seen him?"

"No, but I've seen what he's eaten. Four lettuces munched down to stumps, enough carrot tops to feed a rabbit warren and chewed pea pods scattered everywhere."

As if to prove Ned's point an outraged cry rose from the vegetable patch as Dad discovered the damage.

"How do you know it was Flopper?"

"I found a hole in the fence with tell-tale hairs sticking to the wire. Something white and furry has squeezed through all right."

"At least he's safe," said Natty. "Even if he is going to be the most unpopular rabbit in the universe when Dad finds out it was him."

Ned snorted.

"And the fattest."

"Where shall we look?" Natty asked. "We must find him before he does any more damage."

"I've looked everywhere," said Ned. "Up the runner beans, around the beetroot, between the onions. You name it, I've been there."

"Maybe he's gone to lie down," said Natty.

"I wouldn't be at all surprised."

"Or set off to find his nice cosy hutch."

"To do that he'll have had to squeeze back through the hole."

"Into Penelope's garden," added Natty.

They peeped out just as Dad's boots approached and disappeared above them into the shed. His feet on the planks were deafening so it was a relief when he clomped outside again.

"He's going to dig up the carrots," said Natty, recognizing the garden fork, its prongs as thick as planks, flying above their heads.

"Let's go," said Ned. "The hole's at the bottom of the garden."

He trotted on to the path while Natty kept a lookout for big feet. They cantered to the safety of the rhubarb and paused. A quick glance under the umbrella leaves told them Flopper wasn't there.

Back on the path, Ned set off at a trot but was soon galloping so fast that the wind whistled. It was miles to the bottom of the garden and Natty held on tight.

They were tearing along at a terrific rate, when a missile the size of a tree trunk hurtled from the sky and landed in front of them. Natty ducked while Ned changed pace and jumped it. Another and another fell in quick succession, one behind them and one in front. Ned jumped the one in front, unbalancing Natty, who clung on until the end of the path where they took shelter under some spinach leaves.

"Someone's dropping trees," she said, thoroughly alarmed. Ned got his breath back as another orange missile joined the others on the path.

"Not trees – carrots," he said. "Pity there's no time for a nibble!"

He swung round and trotted on towards the hedge.

In front of them a square wooden structure grew high as a skyscraper. Natty knew it to be Dad's compost bin, full of grass cuttings and vegetable waste. Along the front, at ground level, was a place where one of the wooden slats had rotted,

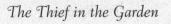

making a hole. Natty noticed it at once because poking from it, testing the air, was a pink nose.

"Look," she whispered. Ned froze into stillness. They watched as a white head emerged, a white head with a pair of floppy ears. "It's him." The rabbit blinked sleepy eyes.

"Well who'd have thought of looking in the compost heap," whispered Ned.

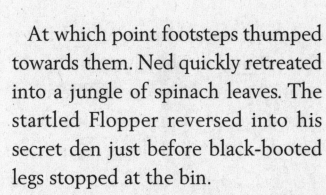

At which point footsteps thumped towards them. Ned quickly retreated into a jungle of spinach leaves. The startled Flopper reversed into his secret den just before black-booted legs stopped at the bin.

Above them, Dad threw a fistful of chewed pea pods on to the heap and raised the garden fork. It flashed down, biting into the earth in front of Flopper's hole. The footsteps clumped away again but the fork stayed put. Flopper was behind bars.

"Dad's trapped him," said Natty. "Without even knowing it."

"And a jolly good thing too," replied Ned. "All we need to do now is get you big again and you can collect him whenever you like."

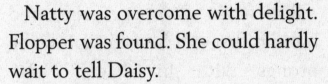

Natty was overcome with delight. Flopper was found. She could hardly wait to tell Daisy.

But Flopper had no intention of remaining a prisoner. He urgently wanted to get out. He sniffed the prongs and tested all the gaps with his whiskers, but it was obvious he was too large to squeeze between any of them. With surprising determination he scrabbled against a prong with his front paws, and when nothing happened, returned into the hole.

"He's caught all right," said Ned.

But when Flopper reappeared bottom first and heaved against the prongs with his back, Natty wondered if Ned was mistaken. At first nothing happened, then slowly the fork toppled.

"Look out!" cried Natty.

As quick as a flash, Ned jumped sideways and for the second time that day Natty ended halfway up his neck.

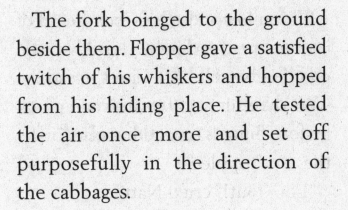
The fork boinged to the ground beside them. Flopper gave a satisfied twitch of his whiskers and hopped from his hiding place. He tested the air once more and set off purposefully in the direction of the cabbages.

"That rabbit's going back for pudding," said Ned.

"I don't suppose he's ever heard of an angry gardener," said Natty, hauling herself back into the saddle. "We'd better get after him and quick before he eats something else."

Chapter 5

The Magician's Hat

Natty had never been frightened of a rabbit before, but then she had never met one five times bigger than she was, at least the size of a rhinoceros. As Ned closed the gap between them, the hopping rabbit appeared to grow larger. Natty couldn't think how to stop him.

"We must get you back to your proper size to catch Flopper," said Ned. "We'll go behind the runner beans. Hold tight."

Ned cantered for the cover of the beans and pulled up, blowing.

"Time to get off," he said.

"What will you do?"

"I'll go back to my picture. You catch that rabbit before he gets into more trouble."

Natty swung herself to the ground.

"Thank you for everything, Ned. Will you keep my riding clothes safe?"

"Of course," said Ned. "There's lots

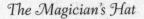

more riding to come. Now go and catch that bunny."

Natty gave Ned a brief hug.

"Goodbye," she said, and let go of the reins. At once the wind bore her away. When she opened her eyes she was her proper size again and Ned had disappeared.

She peeped round the runner beans. Jamie was piling the carrots into a polythene bag. Flopper was inspecting a young cabbage plant and Dad was checking the remaining lettuces. Fortunately, he didn't know there were only the peas between himself and the greedy rabbit thief.

Voices and the sound of the side gate opening distracted everyone, even Flopper. It was Penelope Potter and her cousin Daisy. Penelope looked fed up and Daisy not far from tears. The two girls crossed the grass, stepping round Jamie's magician's hat and cloak which lay in a neglected heap.

A wonderful plan popped into Natty's head. She darted forward, scooped up the surprised rabbit before he took a single bite and, hugging her prize, darted back to her hiding place behind the runner beans. Amazingly, no one noticed.

"Hello, Penelope," said Jamie. "Who's your friend?"

"My cousin, Daisy."

"Hello," said Daisy.

"Isn't Natty with you?" asked Jamie. "We thought you were off riding Pebbles."

"Some chance! No, we're not riding Pebbles and we haven't seen Natty for ages," said Penelope, sniffily. Daisy pulled anxiously at the thin red lead she was carrying.

"We've been looking everywhere for Flopper," she said. Dad straightened up.

"And who may I ask is Flopper?"

"My pet rabbit."

"Your pet what!"

Daisy looked up with wide, startled eyes. It was an awkward moment, saved by Natty who jumped out from her hiding place.

"Hello, Penelope. Hi, Daisy."

"Natty, where've you been?" asked Dad.

"Looking for Flopper." For some reason she was no longer wearing her sweatshirt.

"I keep telling Daisy it's pointless,"

said Penelope. "If we haven't found him by now the fox is bound to have eaten him. They love rabbits, especially juicy ones who are too fat to run away."

Daisy's face crumpled and she took in a deep breath.

"NO!" she wailed. "STOP SAYING that!"

The noise brought Mum hurrying to find out what was wrong and everyone gathered around the unhappy little girl.

"Oh, Daisy, do shut up," said Penelope, embarrassed by all the fuss. "You've got to face facts. We can't find him and that's probably why."

In this noisy confusion Natty reached behind the beans and gently lifted a bundle from the ground before scampering across the grass to collect Jamie's magician's hat and cloak. Hands full, she hurried to the shed and scampered inside. Then she poked her head round the door and shouted above the din.

"Jamie! Come here a minute."

Daisy's cries lessened and everyone turned to look.

"What for?"

"Something peculiar's happened to your magician's hat." Jamie turned to the place where he had last seen it. The fact that it was gone sent him racing.

"What's happened to it?"

"This," said Natty, and pulled him into the shed and closed the door.

From inside came a lot of whispering.

Dad looked at Mum and raised an eyebrow.

He started towards the shed, but was stopped in his tracks when the door burst open and Natty jumped out, tootling a fanfare.

"Taa taddle, ta, ta, taddle, ta, taaaaaa! Ladies and gentlemen. Roll up, roll up, to see the great magician Jamie and his magic hat." Natty clapped for all she was worth. The audience looked surprised, and in Daisy's case, astonished.

With a swirl and a flourish, Jamie stepped from the shed. From under the black cloak he took out his magician's hat and his magic wand.

"Abracadabra, dee diddle dabbit." He waved the wand and tossed it to Natty.

"From out of my magic hat comes. . .

. . .A WHITE RABBIT!"

Triumphant, he lifted out one bemused white bunny. In the pause that followed, Daisy's expression changed from misery to joy.

"FLOPPER!"

she gasped and rushed forwards.

Jamie placed the rabbit in her outstretched arms and the little girl nuzzled her face in his fur, covering him with her curls.

"Well blow me down," said Dad. "The thief in the garden, I presume!"

"Thank goodness for that," said Penelope. "Now we can go riding at last." She beamed at Jamie. "It was awfully clever of you to find him."

"I didn't," said Jamie. "It was Natty. I just did the thing I always wanted to do, pull a rabbit out of my hat. Brilliant!"

Later, when all the excitement had died down and Daisy had introduced Flopper to everyone, even Dad, Natty climbed the stairs to her bedroom. The first thing she saw was Tabitha, still fast asleep on the duvet. She turned to the poster on the wall. Ned gazed out in the direction of the window, without doubt a picture pony again. Natty ran her fingers over the shiny paper and hoped no one would notice that he was not in quite the same position as before.

She lay on the bed and put her arms around Tabitha, stroking the cat's soft nose and fluffy head. Tabitha half opened her eyes and purred.

"I've had an amazing adventure," Natty whispered.

Then she smiled up at Ned. "And I wish more than anything for another one soon!"

The End

Magic Pony

Night-Time Adventure

For my uncle,
R.W.H., with love.

Contents

Chapter 1

A Night-Time Surprise

Natty woke up suddenly and unexpectedly in the dark with something tickling her ear. It felt like the hairy feet of a spider and she quickly brushed it away. The tickling started again on her chin and warm air blew on her cheek. Pressing herself against the wall, she reached

the light switch at last. She laughed
when the light came on. It wasn't a
spider at all. Nothing like.

It was the tickling of pony whiskers and the blowing of warm pony breath. Ned had woken her, the beautiful chestnut pony who lived in the poster pinned to her bedroom wall. His gentle lips wobbled affectionately against her cheek. How lucky she was to have such a secret; her very own magic pony. She rubbed the sleep from her eyes and glanced at the clock on the shelf.

"Hello," said the pony amiably, not seeming to mind that he only just fitted the space between the bed and the wall.

"Ned," said Natty. "It's half past two in the morning. Why aren't you asleep?"

"Now what sort of a greeting is that?" asked the pony. "Do you want me to go back in my picture?"

"No," said Natty, alarmed that he might. Ever since buying this most unusual pony poster from Cosby's Magic Emporium, Natty never quite knew when Ned would come alive. If the magic was happening now she didn't want to waste a moment of it. "It's only that it's the middle of the night. I've never been awake at half past two in the morning before."

"That's the whole point," said Ned. "Everyone in the house is fast asleep, even that cat."

Ned meant Tabitha, Natty's tabby cat, who lay curled up on the duvet. This wasn't quite true, for Natty's wriggling had disturbed her and Tabitha had half an eye open. As for Ned, whether big or small, and he could be either, Tabitha had learnt to ignore him.

"It's the perfect time for jumping practice. So get up and get on."

During the day, when her curtains were drawn open, Natty often watched Penelope Potter jump her pony Pebbles over the blue barrels in the field on the other side of the lane. And now Ned was teaching her to do the same! What did it matter if it was the middle of the night? Natty scrambled from under the duvet, leaving Tabitha to curl into an undisturbed ball.

"I can't ride in pyjamas. I'd better get my jeans on."

"No need for that," said Ned. And of course there wasn't, for the moment Natty sat on Ned's back, the magic would change her pyjamas into riding clothes.

"Where shall we jump?" Natty asked, putting her bare toes into the waiting stirrup and springing on. The pony's reply was drowned in a rushing wind and Natty closed her eyes. When she opened them again, Ned was trotting across a field of brown tuffets which Natty recognized as her carpet. Ned's magic had shrunk them into the tiniest pony and tiniest rider in the world. He rounded the towering height of the door and cantered towards the top of the stairs, guided by the light that spilled from Natty's bedroom.

"Where are we going?" Natty whispered.

"Downstairs, of course," came the reply.

The drop from the landing on to the first stair was huge and the giant steps disappeared into a pit of black. Jumping practice was starting in earnest. Natty clung on, remembering she had gone downstairs like this once before. By the time they reached the hall Natty's eyes were staring pools, desperate to fathom out what lay ahead in the darkness. To her relief she hadn't fallen off. Just as well! Any loud noise would wake Mum, Dad and Jamie, and she certainly didn't want that.

"Get off now," said Ned. "And switch on the living-room light. We'll set up a jumping course in there."

"Oh, yes," said Natty. "I know the very place." She slid to the ground and let go of the reins. The wind spun her until she was her proper size and back in her pyjamas. She tiptoed forward, following the tiny Ned who cantered in front of her as if he were Esmerelda, Prince or

Percy, one of her three china horses come to life. She pushed open the living-room door and switched on the light. Fred the goldfish fluttered into action in his bowl on the shelf, surprised by the sudden brightness. Natty hurried to the table. It was laid ready for breakfast, just how Mum liked it.

"Ned, let's make a jumping course up here. There's loads of things that could be jumps."

"Show me." Natty held out her palms and lifted him.

Ned was soon trotting across the tablecloth, inspecting the breakfast crockery.

"Yes," he said. "The brown sauce bottle, the knives and forks and the salt and pepper pots. We can use all those."

"And the mugs," said Natty. "They can lie on their sides and be pretend barrels. Almost as good as the barrels Penelope Potter has for Pebbles to jump."

"They'll make a mighty jump, mind," said Ned, trotting round one. "The plates are no use. They need to be put to one side."

"My school bag's here," said
Natty, grabbing it from beside a
chair and delving in. "My pens and
pencils can be poles."

She scattered three felt-tips and
two striped pencils on the table and
pulled out her scissors. "What can
my scissors be? I know, they can be

opened out and balanced on their handles. They're blunt as anything so no chance of getting cut – and brilliant as a cross-blade jump. And look, Mum's workbasket is loaded with cotton reels. They can be jump stands."

"Good thinking," said Ned. "As our small selves we'll practise indoors on the table, and as our large selves we'll ride out to Penelope Potter's field and jump Pebbles's barrels."

"In the dark?" exclaimed Natty, already balancing a knife and a fork across the salt and pepper pots.

"It's a full moon tonight," said Ned. "With luck we'll have plenty of light."

Natty darted to the window and pulled back the curtains, knowing Penelope would hate someone else jumping her blue barrels, even if it

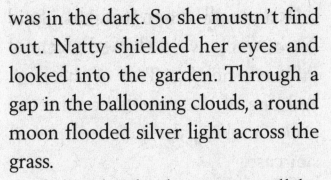
was in the dark. So she mustn't find
out. Natty shielded her eyes and
looked into the garden. Through a
gap in the ballooning clouds, a round
moon flooded silver light across the
grass.

"If the clouds clear away it'll be
perfect," Natty said, looking for stars.
How exciting it would be to do
night-time jumping out of doors.
She returned to the table.

After the salt and pepper pot,
knife and fork jump she opened the
scissors and balanced them on their
handles to make the cross-blade
jump. The mugs were put on their

sides and turned into barrels, and the cotton reels were stacked at three different heights. Two of the pens and one of the pencils became the poles, making the pen and pencil staircase.

Next she turned the sauce bottle on its side to make a wall. And finally, Natty discovered Mum's glasses in the workbasket, opened them out and made three jumps. The spectacles single, if jumped facing the lenses or the spectacles double if the arms were jumped. She bounced over them with her fingers – boing boing! Then she watched enchanted as Ned, mane flying, jumped the whole course.

It was a clear round and Natty hugged her hands to stop herself from clapping – a thing certain to wake the family and bring them downstairs to find out what was going on. Instead her delight was shown by a grin which grew wider as Ned trotted towards her. Leaning back on his haunches, he bowed politely.

"Now it's your turn, Natty. I'll come down to the floor, then you can mount. But we'll need some sort of road to ride up to get us back up here as our small selves."

"I know," said Natty. "If I pull Dad's chair close to the table we can use the rug."

She hurried to show Ned what she meant. After a bit of a struggle, she had the armchair in position with the rug draped over. One end hung from the chair back while Natty stretched the other end out over the seat and weighted it with the legs of the small table.

Now there was a long ramp from the floor to the top of the chair.

"Well done," said Ned, impressed. He jumped on to the rug and galloped all the way down to the floor without there being the slightest sag.

When his feet touched the carpet he was suddenly his big self, wearing

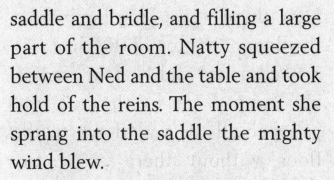

saddle and bridle, and filling a large part of the room. Natty squeezed between Ned and the table and took hold of the reins. The moment she sprang into the saddle the mighty wind blew.

When it stopped she was dressed in her magic riding clothes and was dwarfed by giant furniture. Looking up, her breath was taken away by the vast armchair mountain.

Ned stepped on to the rug ramp cautiously, yet Natty's extra weight made no difference; the rug stayed taut and stretched. The pony trotted briskly all the way to the top and jumped on to the table.

Natty gasped at what she saw. As her big self she thought she had made the showjumps sensibly low; but now she was a tiny rider they looked huge. Most frightening of all were the giant mug barrels – imposingly round and solid and higher than Ned's shoulders.

"This is just the sort of practice course you need," said Ned. "Jump this lot and you'll soon be showing that Penelope Potter what's what."

"Yes," said Natty faintly. It seemed a flock of butterflies had been let loose in her tummy. Right now she didn't care if Penelope Potter could do showjumping better than she could. She wanted to go back to bed.

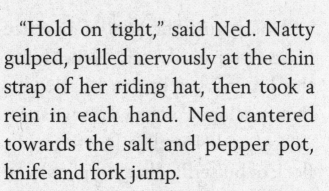

"Hold on tight," said Ned. Natty gulped, pulled nervously at the chin strap of her riding hat, then took a rein in each hand. Ned cantered towards the salt and pepper pot, knife and fork jump.

It was now or never, she could see that.

Chapter 2
Things That Go Bump
in the Night

"Here we go," Ned said. At the last moment Natty grabbed a handful of mane. Ned soared into the air and, leaning into the angle of the jump, Natty went with him. Ned hit the tablecloth on the other side with a thump, and was cantering towards the open scissors

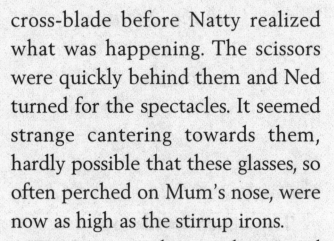
cross-blade before Natty realized what was happening. The scissors were quickly behind them and Ned turned for the spectacles. It seemed strange cantering towards them, hardly possible that these glasses, so often perched on Mum's nose, were now as high as the stirrup irons.

"Don't worry about a thing," said Ned. "Just go with the jump." And he leapt. For a moment Natty caught a glimpse of Ned's legs reflected in the glass, then they were in the air and on the other side, cantering round to the sauce-bottle wall.

The sauce bottle seemed like nothing after the spectacles and even the pen and pencil staircase, which came next, was easy. Ned made a tight turn and suddenly the mug barrels lay ahead, by far the biggest jump. The pony gathered himself up, shortening his stride, and the barrels came closer. Natty concentrated hard and the moment Ned sprang she was ready. Ned cleared the barrels and so did she!

"Well done," he said. Natty was jubilant. It was a clear round.

"I didn't think I could do it but I did. Thank you, Ned." She leaned forward and gave the pony a hug.

"Now it's your turn to steer," said Ned. "You guide me to wherever you want to go."

"All right," said Natty, filled with a glorious sense of achievement. "We'll go round again."

283

So engrossed were they, that neither of them noticed the living-room door open just enough for a curious cat to pad silently in. Neither did they see Tabitha slip under the tablecloth to listen to the unusual thuds coming from above.

Although there was more to think about, Natty found steering fun, and with mounting excitement she turned Ned for the salt and pepper pot, knife and fork jump. They were quickly over it and cantering towards the scissors which they cleared easily, and the sauce-bottle wall, which caused no problems either.

After this, Natty changed the route and swung Ned round to jump the arms of the spectacles. Only when facing them did she realize this was going to be more tricky than she thought.

It was too late to stop. Ned jumped, hit the tablecloth and

jumped again. But it was too quick for Natty. By the second landing she had lost her balance. As Ned slowed to help her, the tablecloth suddenly shifted and an unexpected, furry giant landed in front of them.

"Stupid cat!" Ned shouted, swerving sharply. "Get off the table!"

Now nothing could stop Natty, and she and Ned parted company. In a split second Natty grew to her proper size and landed in the middle of the table. There was a terrible rattling of crockery and all the showjumps collapsed. Tabitha dived for the floor; Ned for the safety of the rug ramp. Unable to stop herself, Natty slid, pulling the tablecloth, breakfast things and showjumps off the table with her.

The crash and clatter was startling and landing with a surprised grunt amongst the debris, Natty sat stunned.

Then, from the corner of her eye,
she saw the alarmed Fred swimming
round and round in his bowl.

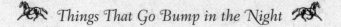

"Sorry, Fred," she said. "No need to panic." Then she realized that after a crash like that there was every need to panic. She looked round quickly for Ned. Both he and Tabitha had disappeared. Just as well, she thought. Mindful that she had bare feet, she unwrapped herself from the tablecloth and hurriedly surveyed the damage.

It wasn't as bad as she expected. One plate in two halves, green felt-tip on the tablecloth, the handle of her own special mug snapped off. The rest a tangle that needed sorting. She started at once. With luck she could have the table set again before the mess was discovered. Working quickly, she started to pile up the plates and didn't see the tall, slow-moving figure creep in from the hall – with a big, black boot held up at the ready.

"Natty! What do you think you're doing?"

She nearly jumped out of her skin.

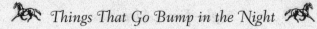

"Dad!" Behind Dad was Jamie, pale and wide-eyed, brandishing the magic wand from his conjuring set.

"You really frightened me!" she gasped.

"Us frighten *you*? What sort of a fright do you think you gave us? We thought you were a burglar. Your mother's under the duvet, all of a quiver," said Dad.

"No, I'm not," said Mum. "I just had to get my dressing-gown on." Even Mum was clasping a wooden coat-hanger to her chest. "I couldn't meet a burglar in my nightie."

"Oh," said Natty.

"Yes," said Jamie. "We were going to tie you up and hand you over to the police."

"Humph!" said Dad, dropping the boot in the hall. "That won't be necessary now we know it was you."

"I'm sorry to wake you," said Natty. "I had a bit of an accident with the tablecloth. Well, it was Tabitha. She got on the table and, well, her claws pulled it and, well, everything came off." It was the best truth she could manage and Natty hoped that it would do.

"But what were you doing down

here at this time of night?" Dad asked. "It's gone three o'clock. You should be fast asleep." Natty held up her broken mug with one hand and crossed her fingers behind her back with the other.

"I came to fetch a mug of water and now I've broken it. Sorry."

Fortunately Tabitha chose this moment to come out from behind the sofa and brush herself around Natty's legs.

"Honestly, that cat's more trouble than she's worth," said Mum. "Come on, we can leave the mess until morning. Back to bed everyone."

But Natty realized she couldn't leave everything until the morning. There were pens and pencils, cotton reels and scissors muddled in with the crockery. She needed to tidy them away to avoid anyone asking more awkward questions.

"Leave everything." Mum was firm. "Find a mug with a handle and fill it. Then it's straight up to bed."

Dad shook his head. "Accidents will happen, I suppose," he said.

297

"Excitement over, Jamie. Back to bed now. It's a school day tomorrow."

When Natty came from the kitchen carrying her water, she looked quickly round for Ned. He was nowhere to be seen, thank goodness, although she longed to know where he'd got to. Mum's hand on her shoulder steered her from the living room.

"Can we leave the door open for Tabitha?" Natty asked.

"I suppose so," said Mum, switching off the light. "Now upstairs at once. In future remember to take up water with you when you go to bed. We don't want a repeat performance of tonight, thank you very much."

Natty plodded up the stairs with her mug clasped in both hands. She stopped at the top.

"If I was a burglar would you have bashed me with the coat-hanger?"

With twinkling eyes, Mum waved it.

"If you'd been stealing my favourite flower vase – yes! Now hurry back to bed."

Natty turned into her bedroom and checked to see if Ned was back in his poster. He wasn't. She put the mug beside her clock, flopped on to the duvet with a sigh, and switched off the light. It's lucky Mum and Dad don't seem cross so far, she thought. But the kind of accident they *think* I've had is one thing.

Showjumping on the table is quite another. If they find *that* out, then they'll be cross. She covered her knees with the duvet.

When everyone had gone back to sleep she would find Ned and sort the showjumps from the rest of the crockery on the floor.

Chapter 3
The Moon Shines Bright

It was difficult trying to stay awake. Natty propped herself against the wall but soon her head nodded forward. When her chin knocked her chest she opened her eyes and shook herself, but the effect didn't last long. Her eyelids drooped and down went her chin again. This time she didn't wake.

It was Tabitha landing on the duvet, purring loudly and brushing her body against Natty's sagging knees that finally roused her.

"Mmm, mmm, what?" Slowly she awoke. "Tabby?" she said, and wrapped her arms around the warm furry bundle. The purring grew even louder. Natty would have dropped off again if Tabitha hadn't licked the back of her hand. The rasping sound and prickly sensation woke her properly, and remembering what she had to do she felt along the shelf for her pocket torch.

"This time, Tabby, you stay here," whispered Natty. She shone the torch at the clock. A quarter to four! Then on to Ned's poster. Empty. She listened hard and, although Tabitha was still purring, the rest of the house seemed quiet and still. She climbed cautiously out of bed, tiptoed to the window and lifted back the curtain.

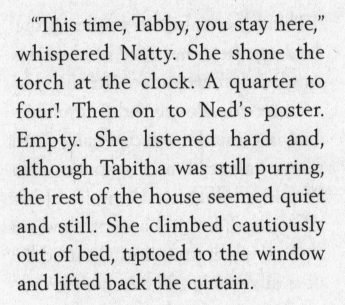

The sky was full of stars and the field on the other side of the lane was flooded with moonlight.

Esmerelda, Prince and Percy stood in a line on the window sill. They seemed to stare at the spot where Penelope Potter's pony Pebbles stood, head up, ears pricked, a shining silver statue in the middle of a silver lake. Natty craned her neck to see what he was looking at. Whatever it was was way out of view and she didn't dare open the window in case it made a noise.

She let the curtain fall; she had important things to see to. She squeezed round her bedroom door, and turning the handle bit by bit closed it without a sound, leaving Tabitha shut in. The torch lit her way along the landing and down the stairs.

Natty paused at the bottom and listened. Silence! More confident, she tiptoed into the living room. She pushed the door to and put on the light to see the tiny Ned canter across the carpet towards her.

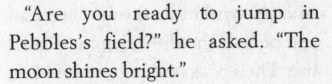

"Are you ready to jump in Pebbles's field?" he asked. "The moon shines bright."

Natty longed to say yes, longed to ride out into the shimmering world of Pebbles's field, but first things had to come first.

"I can't," she said. "Not until I've tidied up the jumping things."

She put her torch in her pyjama bottoms pocket and started her search amongst the wreckage. She closed the scissors, grateful that she hadn't sat on them, and found the spectacles in one piece, which was a relief. She picked out the cotton reels and tidied them back into

Mum's workbasket, and the pens and pencils she shoved in her school bag. There was nothing she could do about the green blob of felt-tip on the tablecloth but it wasn't a very big blob, so with luck no one would notice it.

"There," said Natty. "All done. I'll have to leave the cutlery and other stuff on the floor otherwise it'll be obvious I got up again. Lucky no one noticed the rug over the chair. I could never have explained that." She laid it out carefully on the floor and pulled Dad's armchair back into place.

"It was unfortunate about that cat," said Ned. "The jumping was going well until she arrived."

"Never mind," said Natty. "She can't follow us this time. I've shut her in my bedroom."

"Good," said Ned. "You'd better put something on your feet."

"My wellies! They're by the back door. Let's go out that way and round by the side gate."

Natty switched out the light and with the torch, shone the way to the kitchen. Here she pulled on her wellington boots and unlocked the back door.

The tiny pony jumped from the step and Natty followed him out into the night.

Nothing stirred. A barn owl hooted in Winchway Wood and above them twinkled a million distant stars. But most enchanting of all, Natty thought, was to see Ned, standing before her on the grass, a proper pony size, tacked up and ready for her to mount.

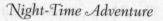
Showjumping by moonlight! What could be more thrilling?

"Penelope Potter'd be furious if she found out I'd used her jumps without asking," whispered Natty, as with shining eyes she took hold

of the reins and sprang on to Ned's back. Wellingtons and pyjamas disappeared and she was transformed into a rider with velvet hard hat, hacking jacket, jodhpurs and jodhpur boots.

"Penelope Potter will never ever find out," whispered back Ned.

How silly to think that in such wonderful clothes and riding such a handsome chestnut pony that Penelope Potter had a chance of recognizing her. Of course she didn't.

Natty chuckled with excitement as Ned walked across the grass and round the side of the house to the gate. She leaned forward and lifted the latch. Ned backed away so she could pull the gate open and then they were in the lane.

"Ready to go?" asked Ned.

Natty was ready for anything, which was just as well. For instead of letting Natty open the field gate, Ned trotted a little way down the lane, turned and cantered straight for it. He put in a huge leap and they were in the field before the gasp of surprise had left Natty's lips.

"Well sat," said Ned. "In spite of that unfortunate tumble earlier I can

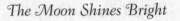

see that you haven't lost your nerve."

"You didn't give me a chance to think about it," said Natty.

"After the gate, jumping Pebbles's barrels will be nothing." And her eyes searched the field for the dappled grey pony. "That's funny. Where is Pebbles? He was here a little while ago. I saw him from my window."

"Well, he's not here now," said Ned.

With a jolt Natty remembered Pebbles's fixed look in the direction of Penelope's stable yard, and felt a sudden stab of anxiety.

Across the still night air and from the direction of the yard came the long, lonely whinny of a confused and worried pony. It was answered by a voice Natty had never heard before. Its low, cross tones struck a chill in her heart. She could just make out the words.

"Get on in horse, else you'll regret it."

Chapter 4
Thieves in the Night

Above the stable roof, the moonlight lit up the flat top of a lorry. Natty froze with fear, but Ned hurried into action and she clung on.

"Don't say a word," he whispered, and keeping in the shadow of the hedge, they trotted towards

Penelope's stable yard, Ned's unshod feet swishing through the grass, beating out a soft rhythm. From the yard came the hollow clatter of pony feet climbing up a horsebox ramp.

Natty knew the sound from when Penelope loaded Pebbles into his pony trailer, only this time it wasn't Penelope. Penelope was tucked up fast asleep in bed. Someone else was loading Pebbles; someone up to no good.

"We've got to stop them," she whispered in Ned's ear. "They're stealing Pebbles!"

"Don't worry," Ned whispered back. "We will." And he broke into a steady canter, charging through the open gate into the stable yard where he galloped towards the lorry and straight into a rushing wind. Ned and Natty went from big to small in a moment and disappeared between the front wheels of the lorry just as a pair of trousered legs ran alongside it.

"What was that?" The cross voice again. "I swear there was only one pony in the field. Was that another?"

Now a younger voice.

"No boss, I didn't see anything."

"Close up the ramp and get in the cab. We got to clear out of here. That grey animal's made noise enough to wake the dead."

One pair of legs disappeared towards the front of the lorry, the other pair ran for the back. Ned galloped from between the rear wheels, swung round and jumped on to the ramp. Up he galloped, leaping each anti-slip bar like a racehorse, his rider bent double like a jockey. Natty glanced over her shoulder in time to see the accomplice thief start lifting.

The ramp straightened under them and Ned half-jumped, half-fell into the lorry. It banged closed behind them and they were left in pitch black. Pebbles, upset by the rough treatment he had received, cried out with an ear-splitting whinny that only faded when the engine broke into a roar. The lorry swung out of the yard and drove off, nearly knocking Ned from his feet.

"Natty, are you all right?" Ned asked, his sides heaving as he regained his breath.

"Yes, but I can't see a thing."
Wondering if her torch would have
transferred itself from her pyjamas
to her jodhpurs, she fumbled in the
little pocket near the waistband.
What a relief to find it was there!

"Shine it ahead," said Ned. "I need
to see where Pebbles's feet are."

The wobbly pinprick of light picked out Pebbles's four great hooves, one after the other, enabling Ned to make his way shakily across the juddering rubber matting.

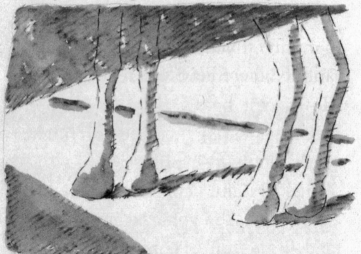

"Got my bearings now," said Ned. "Hold tight and crouch right down."

A whirl of wind spun them and in a moment Ned was as big as Pebbles and Natty found herself ducking down just below the lorry's roof. Pebbles peered into the torchlight with a look of surprise.

"It's all right, Pebbles. It's only us," said Natty. "I'm going to get off Ned and untie you." Pebbles whickered with relief; friends had arrived.

"Easy does it, Natty," said Ned.

"And keep hold of my reins." Natty slid to the ground between the two ponies, who now stood side by side. She looped Ned's reins over her arm and edged towards Pebbles's head. Ned rested his muzzle in a comforting way on the grey pony's neck while Natty untied the halter rope. As soon as he could, Pebbles nuzzled Natty's arm before turning to Ned. The two ponies blew a nose-to-nose greeting in the way that horses do.

"Now what?" asked Natty, grabbing a handful of Ned's mane as the lorry lurched round a bend.

"We get the thieves to stop," said
Ned. "And we do it like this."

To Natty's surprise Ned's back end

lifted into the air and both
hind legs kicked hard against the
side of the lorry. Everything swayed.

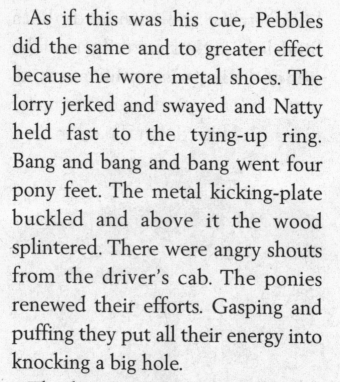

As if this was his cue, Pebbles did the same and to greater effect because he wore metal shoes. The lorry jerked and swayed and Natty held fast to the tying-up ring. Bang and bang and bang went four pony feet. The metal kicking-plate buckled and above it the wood splintered. There were angry shouts from the driver's cab. The ponies renewed their efforts. Gasping and puffing they put all their energy into knocking a big hole.

The lorry came to a spluttering, lurching stop and the floor ended up angled to one side.

"Looks like we've ended up in a ditch," said Ned cheerily, as if he couldn't have wished for anything better. "Get on, Natty, and get ready to lead Pebbles down the ramp."

Pebbles, meanwhile, kept up the kicking with one leg, needing his other three to balance. Natty had just enough space. It was the first time she had mounted from this side, and using her right foot was awkward until she found herself pushed from underneath by Ned's nose.

Once in the saddle she crouched low to avoid hitting her head on the roof. She had a firm hold of Pebbles's lead rope with one hand; the other held tight to Ned's mane. This was the most scary thing she had ever done and she took a deep breath to quieten her pounding heart.

Bang and bang and bang, went Pebbles. Chunks of wood flew and there were angry shouts at the back of the lorry.

"Get ready," said Ned, turning to face the ramp. "As soon as this thing goes down we leave."

The lock unclicked. Bang, bang went Pebbles for good measure. A slit of moonlight appeared and the ramp started to go down. Pebbles got in two more kicks and Ned coiled under Natty like a spring.

"All right, you stupid horse," said a brawny figure, springing towards them. "You've asked for it."

"Charge!" yelled Natty at the top of her voice and Ned leapt forwards. The astonished horse thief tumbled backwards.

Natty had the satisfaction of seeing him splash into the ditch as Ned clattered down the chaotically bouncing ramp, followed by an eager Pebbles. Then with a sound like gunfire, a hinge snapped. The terrified accomplice dived for the safety of the hedge as not one pony but two jumped to safety and cantered off down the moonlit road.

"That's given them something to think about," said Ned. "Stuck in a ditch with the ramp hanging half off. The lorry won't be going anywhere like that. It's well and truly stranded."

"Good," grinned the triumphant Natty, holding tight to Pebbles's lead rope. "They won't be stealing any more ponies tonight, that's for sure."

Behind them furious shouts faded into the distance.

Chapter 5

Mystery Rider

Pebbles's hooves hammered the road's hard surface and mingled with the duller beat of Ned's unshod feet. The further they raced, the more Natty was sure a beat was missing. But there was nothing wrong with Pebbles – he cantered easily beside her – and

Ned was fine too. In the end Natty forgot to listen as she tried to work out where they were.

The ponies put in a good distance between themselves and the stranded thieves before slowing. Hot and blowing, they stopped for a rest. The moon seemed to shed less light and the sky was paler. Natty wondered how long they had been travelling and how far they had come.

"Well," said Ned. "Where do we go from here?"

"I'm not sure!" Natty tried desperately to find a recognizable landmark. But the moonlit countryside looked so different from how she usually saw it. "We haven't gone by any turnings so we must have come along this road in the lorry. Best to carry on until I work it out."

The ponies started walking and the uneven sound from Pebbles's feet – three clops and a pat – became obvious. Natty finally understood the problem.

"Pebbles has lost a shoe!"

"Wrenched off with all that kicking, no doubt," said Ned. "It's lucky he's not gone lame." But there was no sign of Pebbles limping. On the contrary, he pulled to go forward. Ahead, the moon hung above a line of dark trees, and behind them was a spire.

"I know where we are!" cried Natty, and she realized Pebbles did too. "Not far from home. This is our village. That's the church."

They set off at a trot, coming into Main Street, clattering past the shop, the petrol station and the bus-stop. All familiar signs of home.

"Here's our lane," said Natty. "That's the front entrance to Penelope's house." She pointed to a smart white gate facing on to the main road. "But mostly the Potters use the other entrance. The back drive that comes out opposite the stable yard. The once-upon-a-time stables behind the house are garages now. That's why Pebbles has a new stable in his field."

They swung into the lane and Natty had high hopes of being able to turn Pebbles out without anyone seeing them. But torchlight suddenly lit up the lane and two

figures emerged from the Potters'
back drive.

"Now what are we going to do?" she whispered. "It's Mr Potter and Penelope. They've heard us coming."

"Talk your way out of it. You can do it," whispered back Ned.

"What happens if they recognize me?"

"They won't," Ned assured her.

"Excuse me, that's my pony you've got there!" said Penelope, arms outstretched to stop them passing. "Hand him over."

"That's enough, Penelope. Just leave this to me," said Mr Potter.

"Now, young lady. What are you doing with my daughter's pony, and what for that matter are you doing out at this time of night?"

Natty leaned down and dropped Pebbles's halter rope into Penelope's waiting hand. "I was bringing him back. He's been stolen."

"We know that," said Penelope. "I heard him whinnying. I saw the thieves' lorry drive off up the lane."

Mr Potter looked puzzled.

"How did you find him?" he asked. "The police are out searching right now."

Terrified they'd recognize her voice, the words tumbled out in a rush.

"He escaped from the horsebox. It's stuck in a ditch with a broken ramp. Turn left at the top of the lane and keep on till you find it. Tell the police that. Oh, and he's lost a back shoe." Her legs gave Ned a squeeze. "Goodbye." Ned sprang forwards.

"Now just a minute, young lady," cried Mr Potter, but he was distracted by Pebbles trying to go with them. Mr Potter had to help Penelope hang on tight and in doing so neither of them saw Ned turn at

Natty's house and jump the side gate. The girl rider and the pony had vanished by the time Pebbles was calm again.

Quickly, Ned reached the back garden and Natty slid from his back.

"Thank you, Ned, for saving Pebbles and for the wonderful indoor showjumping." She gave him a quick hug and let go of the reins. At once she was back in her pyjamas and wellies.

She pushed the back door open. Ned tossed his mane and in a moment was his tiny self, leaping up the doorstep into the house. Natty hurried after him, locking the door and kicking off her boots as she went. She caught Ned up on the landing, highlighting him in her torch beam as he pranced, waiting for her.

"Goodbye, Natty, until next time."
The tiny pony voice was a drift of
tinkling bells.

"Goodbye, Ned. It's been the most
exciting night of my life!" came her
whispered reply. She pushed open
her bedroom door and the miniature
pony galloped ahead.

By the time Natty had crept inside, Ned was safely back in his poster. She switched off her torch. Daylight was creeping between her curtains; it was nearly morning. She wriggled her feet under the sleeping Tabitha and looked up at Ned's picture.

"Night night, Magic Pony," she sighed.

"I hope next time will be soon." And she lay down. She sat up again almost at once. "How typical! Penelope didn't even say thank you."

Then, with a sigh of exhaustion, she flopped down again. The next thing she knew she was being shaken awake by Jamie.

"Mum says you've got to get up now," he said. "What's the matter with you? Why didn't you wake up? She's called and called. Now you've missed breakfast."

"Why? What time is it?"

"Quarter to eight!" said Jamie and left her groaning. Natty thought she must be the weariest person in the world. She looked up at Ned in his poster, and slowly the details of last night's adventure came back: showjumping on the table, the shambles on the living-room floor, and saving Pebbles. Tabitha slid off the bed, stretched and trotted off to find her breakfast.

Natty staggered out of bed and, after flinging on her school clothes, arrived in the kitchen with enough time to grab her lunch-box.

"About time too, Natty," said Mum, handing it over. "I've put an extra sandwich in for you to eat on the bus. Now hurry."

"Thanks, Mum." Natty grabbed her school bag from the living room and ran.

She turned the corner at the end of the lane, and saw Penelope talking excitedly to Jamie by the school bus-stop and, for once, he appeared to be listening.

"Amazing," she heard him say as she drew close. "Hey, Natty, guess what happened to Pebbles?"

"I'll tell if you don't mind, Jamie," said Penelope. "He is my pony."

"What?" asked Natty, pretending not to know.

"In the middle of the night he got stolen!" Before Natty could think how to react Penelope went on. "It was weird. We got him back again. But not from the police. From this mystery rider. We heard ponies coming down the lane and there was this girl, terribly smart, on a super chestnut, leading Pebbles. She told us where the thieves' lorry was, handed Pebbles over and vanished! And she was right. The police caught the thieves trying to pull their lorry out of a ditch with a stolen tractor. Only nobody seems to know who she was. Don't you think that's extraordinary?"

Natty blinked and nodded.

"Yes, and another amazing thing. The thieves tried to say they hadn't stolen Pebbles. But the police found his lost shoe in their lorry and then they got terribly confused about whether they'd stolen one pony or two. All rather peculiar, don't you think?"

Natty opened her mouth to reply, but was saved from having to by the arrival of the school bus. The three of them climbed aboard and Natty sank thankfully into a seat, grateful her secret was safe and delighted the thieves had been caught. Now Penelope had a new audience for her story and told it all over again to anyone on the bus who would listen. At the next stop, Penelope's special friend Trudi got on, so she had to be told too. Left alone, Natty smiled quietly to herself, ate her sandwich and made up an exciting pretend to keep herself awake.

In it she and Ned soared over Pebbles's blue barrels at last.

The End